To Catherine, Emily and Matthew, for your constant inspiration.
To Tony, for your love and support.
To Mom and Dad, for encouraging me in all that I do . . .
How will I ever thank you enough?
—D.R.F.

To my dear sister Vicky (hope she likes the toys!)
—C.M.

Library of Congress Cataloging-in-Publication Data Available

2 4 6 8 10 9 7 5 3 1

Published by Sterling Publishing Co., Inc.
387 Park Avenue South, New York, NY 10016
© 2005 by Della Ross Ferreri
Illustrations © 2005 by Capucine Mazille
Designed by Randall Heath
Distributed in Canada by Sterling Publishing
c/o Canadian Manda Group, 165 Dufferin Street
Toronto, Ontario, Canada M6K 3H6
Distributed in Great Britain and Europe by Chris Lloyd at Orca Book
Services, Stanley House, Fleets Lane, Poole BH15 3AJ, England

Sterling ISBN 1-4027-1492-0

For information about custom editions, special sales, premium and
corporate purchases, please contact Sterling Special Sales
Department at 800-805-5489 or specialsales@sterlingpub.com.

How Will I Ever Sleep in This Bed?

By Della Ross Ferreri

Illustrated by

Capucine Mazille

Sterling Publishing Co., Inc.
New York

I'm big enough now for a bed of my own.
But this bed is enormous! I feel all alone.

I search for my friends in the yellow toy box. Oh, look! Here's my rabbit, my skunk, and my fox!

I stand on my tiptoes and reach
for my dogs.
     And
        down
           come
              my turtles,
                 my fish,
                    and my frogs.

I peek in my closet. Is anyone there?
Oh, good! I see two kangaroos and a bear!

I tuck in my tiger. I cover my sheep.
I tell all my animals, "Now go to sleep!"

A hug for my hippo.
A kiss for my cow.

I guess I can try to squeeze in here somehow.

With frogs at my feet and a horse on my head—oh, how will I ever sleep in this bed?

Move over, monkey. Fly away, bee.
I love all of you, but I need room for me!

So please Mr. Moose
and Blue Dinosaur . . .

You guys are so big.
Can you sleep on the floor?

I pull up my blanket
and wiggle in tight.
Now I feel warm . . .
and snuggly . . .
and sleepy . . .

Good night!